SPOTLIGHT ON NATURE

KOALA

MELISSA GISH

CREATIVE EDUCATION · CREATIVE PAPERBACKS

Published by Creative Education and Creative Paperbacks
P.O. Box 227, Mankato, Minnesota 56002
Creative Education and Creative Paperbacks are imprints
of The Creative Company
www.thecreativecompany.us

Design by Chelsey Luther; production by Joe Kahnke
Art direction by Rita Marshall
Printed in the United States of America

Photographs by Alamy (imageBROKER, Juniors Bildarchiv GmbH, Life on
white, Gerry Pearce, John Quixley), Dreamstime (Pawel Papis), Freevec-
tormaps.com, Getty Images (Andrew Merry/Moment, picture alliance),
iStockphoto (Greg Bethmann, CraigRJD, eeqmcc, StephaneDebove),
Minden Pictures (Sean Crane, D. Parer & E. Parer-Cook, Suzi Eszterhas,
Suzi Eszterhas/NPL, Paul Hobson/NPL, Mitsuaki Iwago, Juergen & Chris-
tine Sohns), Newscom (CB2/ZOB/Supplied by WENN), San Diego Zoo,
Shutterstock (covenant, dan_locke, Robyn Mackenzie, Maridav, Melbourne
Jun PD, Victor Yong)

Library of Congress Cataloging-in-Publication Data
Names: Gish, Melissa, author.
Title: Koala / Melissa Gish.
Series: Spotlight on nature.
Includes index.
Summary: A detailed chronology of developmental milestones drives this life
study of koalas, including their habitats, physical features, and conservation
measures taken to protect these arboreal marsupials.
Identifiers: LCCN 2019060156 / ISBN 978-1-64026-341-3 (hardcover)
/ ISBN 978-1-62832-873-8 (pbk) / ISBN 978-1-64000-482-5 (eBook)
Subjects: LCSH: Koala—Juvenile literature.
Classification: LCC QL737.M384 G57 2021 / DDC 599.2/5—dc23

First Edition HC 9 8 7 6 5 4 3 2 1
First Edition PBK 9 8 7 6 5 4 3 2 1

CONTENTS

KOALAS
of Werrikimbe National Park

Some of the nearly 50 wildlife preserves and national parks comprising the Gondwana Rainforests of Australia are located in the state of New South Wales. One park, Werrikimbe, covers more than 128 square miles (332 sq km) of subtropical rainforest and rivers. Flying foxes, bowerbirds, and colorful parrots fill the treetops. Tree frogs and carpet pythons inhabit the park's wetlands and woods. A variety of Werrikimbe's animals are found on no other continent.

It is mid-December, early summer, and a pleasant 70 °F (21.1 °C). A female koala, perched on a branch 20 feet (6.1 m) above the forest floor, munches the leaves of a snow gum tree. Thirty-five days have passed since she mated. The experienced mother hardly notices as she gives birth to a single offspring. About the size of a jelly bean, the baby joey still has a lot of growing to do.

CLOSE-UP
Eyes

Koalas' eyes have vertically slit pupils that allow koalas to see colors, even in low light. It also helps them spot movement off to the sides, aiding in escape from predators.

CHAPTER ONE
LIFE BEGINS

Koalas are a type of marsupial. Unlike other mammals, marsupials give birth to undeveloped babies, called joeys. After birth, joeys firmly latch on to their mother's nipples and drink milk while continuing to develop. The mother's nipples may be under a flap of skin or inside a pouch, called a marsupium, which holds the joeys. Among marsupials, only the females have a marsupium, but South America's short-tailed opossums lack this protective pouch altogether. About 80 percent of the world's marsupial species are found in Australia, New Guinea, and neighboring islands.

Koalas typically give birth to a single joey. Twins are rare. A new-born koala is just 0.8 inch (2 cm) long. It has no fur, and its hind legs,

**DAY ① **

- ▸ Born
- ▸ Pink-skinned and hairless
- ▸ Crawls from birth canal to pouch
- ▸ Length: 0.8 inch (2 cm)

ears, and eyes are not fully formed. Using its tiny claws, it relies on its well-developed sense of smell to find its way from the birth canal to its mother's pouch. Once inside, the joey will feed on a constant supply of milk for six months. The koala's marsupium opens straight out like a belly button. A strong muscle at the top of the pouch keeps it closed. When the joey is grown, it will push its way out of the pouch. As a youngster, it will ride on its mother's back or rest against her chest.

— FEATURED FAMILY —

Welcome to the World

In Werrikimbe, the joey's claws look like tiny specks of clear glass. His pink skin is thin and fragile, like wet paper. Unable to see or hear, the joey instinctively climbs upward over his mother's dense fur. When he reaches the right position on his mother's belly, her marsupium opens just enough for the little joey to slip inside. Surrounded by the soft, fleshy lining of the pouch, the joey will stay safe and warm as he grows.

3 MONTHS

- Eyes and ears develop
- Fur appears
- Length: 4 inches (10.2 cm)
- Weight: 4 ounces (113 g)

5 MONTHS

- Eyes open
- Pokes head out of pouch for first time
- Length: 5.5 inches (14 cm)
- Weight: 9 ounces (255 g)

Koalas are found in eastern and southeastern Australia. It was once believed that the koalas in different regions were different species. However, genetic studies have shown that there is only one koala species, with adaptations present. Koalas grow to be two to three feet (0.6–0.9 m) long. Those in Queensland are called northern koalas. They are gray with white underbellies. Males average 16 pounds (7.3 kg), and females weigh around 11 pounds (5 kg). Koalas in New South Wales, Victoria, and South Australia are called southern koalas. These koalas have adapted to the continent's colder southern winters. They have thicker, darker brown fur. Males typically weigh about 26 pounds (11.8 kg) and females about 19 pounds (8.6 kg).

CLOSE-UP
Teeth

Two pairs of sharp front teeth clip leaves. Back teeth shred food. A gap between the front and back teeth, called the diastema, allows the tongue to move the mass of leaves around in the mouth as the koala chews.

— FEATURED FAMILY —

First Meal

The Werrikimbe koala joey feeds on his mother's milk. Immunoglobulins in the milk have kept the joey healthy. The mother koala's milk changes as the joey grows. The amount of protein increases when it's time for the joey's brain to develop. Protein drops in favor of fat, once the joey's other organs develop. Week by week, as the joey matures, his mother's body produces different nutritional formulas to help him become a strong, smart koala.

NORTHERN
KOALA
RANGE ●

Koalas are found in
eastern and **southeastern**

AUSTRALIA.

SOUTHERN
KOALA
RANGE ●

⑥ MONTHS

- ▸ Covered with dense fur
- ▸ Teeth have erupted
- ▸ Eats pap to prepare gut

- ▸ Length: 6.5 inches (16.5 cm)
- ▸ Weight: 1 pound (454 g)

CLOSE-UP

Support system

Eleven pairs of ribs and a curved spine
allow a koala to tightly curl its body.
A thick pad made of hard tissue protects
the koala's rump as it sits in tree forks.

CHAPTER TWO

EARLY ADVENTURES

Koalas are folivores, meaning they eat only leaves. The leaves they eat come from eucalyptus, or gum, trees native to Australia. Of the hundreds of eucalyptuses, only about three dozen make up the koala's diet. Eucalyptus leaves are deadly to most other animals. The leaves are also high in fiber, which means it takes a lot of them to provide adequate nutrition. Joeys get their first taste of leaves around eight months old. As adults, they will typically eat more than two pounds (0.9 kg) of leaves per day. Leaves may be stuffed into cheek pouches as snacks to be eaten at a later time.

To conserve energy, koalas spend between 18 and 20 hours per day sleeping while their food digests. Koalas have a specialized digestive system that contains a long sac called a cecum (*SEE-kum*).

8 MONTHS
- No longer fits in pouch
- Carried on mother's back
- Nibbles leaves
- Length: 9 inches (22.9 cm)
- Weight: 2.7 pounds (1.2 kg)

9.5 MONTHS
- Begins drinking less milk
- Eats 5 ounces (142 g) of leaves per day

CLOSE-UP

Preparation pap

Koala mothers produce a soupy substance called pap. Eating pap helps the joey prepare for a life-time of leafy lunches. Pap is rich with microflora to populate the youngster's developing cecum.

— FEATURED FAMILY —

Look Who's Lunching

Now six months old, the Werrikimbe koala joey is covered with soft fur. He looks like a miniature version of his mother. The joey pokes his head out of the pouch and looks around. The sun is shining, and the air feels crisp. He leans down to his mother's lower belly and begins licking a substance secreted by her body. He needs to eat this substance, called pap, before he can begin eating leaves. For the first time in his life, the joey climbs completely out of the pouch. Gripping his mother's fur, he clambers up her chest and wraps his spindly arms around her neck. Now he can see the vast world around him.

KOALAS spend
between **18** and **20** hours per day *sleeping.*

11 MONTHS	**12.5** MONTHS
▸ Eats 8 ounces (227 g) of leaves per day ▸ Length: 11.5 inches (29.2 cm) ▸ Weight: 5.7 pounds (2.6 kg)	▸ No longer drinks milk ▸ Length: 13 inches (33 cm) ▸ Weight: 7.5 pounds (3.4 kg)

Millions of bacteria called microflora live inside the cecum. Their function is to destroy the eucalypt poison and break down the fibrous material, extracting every nutrient possible. Koalas eat from a different tree every day. Sometimes they leap from tree to tree, but more often, they walk. When they are on the ground, koalas are vulnerable to predators such as dogs, dingoes, and goannas. At more than eight feet (2.4 m) long, the tree-climbing perentie—Australia's largest lizard—is also a major threat.

— FEATURED FAMILY —

Give It a Try

The koala mother uses her front teeth to snip off a leaf. Because her paws grip the tree, she cannot use them to push the food into her mouth. Instead, she uses her cheek muscles and tongue to bring the leaf into her mouth. Mimicking his mother, the eight-month-old joey snips the corner of a leaf. But he hasn't yet figured out how to use his tongue to pull the leaf inside his mouth, and it falls to the ground. This will take some practice.

CLOSE-UP
Paws and claws

Each front paw has three fingers and two thumbs. Long, sharp claws and rough pads aid in tree climbing. Each back paw has a clawless thumb and four clawed toes. Two of the toes are fused together and used like a comb to groom fur.

CLAWLESS THUMB

JOINED DIGITS

PAD

DOUBLE THUMBS

(18) MONTHS
- ▸ Leaves mother's group
- ▸ Moves from place to place

(2) YEARS
- ▸ Attempts to settle with new group
- ▸ Chased out by dominant male

CLOSE-UP
Smelling danger

Koalas have a powerful sense of smell.
They rely on their large, leathery noses to
detect different levels of toxins in gum
leaves. They also identify scent warnings
rubbed on trees by other koalas.

CHAPTER THREE

LIFE LESSONS

Koalas have a unique social structure. They like to live alone, but they also share space with one another. A group of koalas living in a particular area is called a colony. After young koalas are weaned, females tend to stay in their mother's colony. Males leave the colony when they are about two years old. They become travelers, roaming from place to place as they look for food and mates. Most of the time, koalas move about freely and stay out of each other's way. But during mating season, from August to early March, males establish territories, claiming certain trees that they refuse to share with other males.

Male koalas secrete an oily substance from a gland on the chest. They rub this oil, called musk, on trees. The stinky, cheesy scent tells other males that a territory is taken. Males also make a sound like a

(3) YEARS

> Fully mature
> Continues to roam various colonies
> Length: 3 feet (0.9 m)
> Weight: 26 pounds (11.8 kg)

This Is How It's Done

In Werrikimbe, early morning dew has formed on leaves. The koala joey and his mother lick the cool moisture. Koalas get 90 percent of the water they need from the leaves they eat. Only during extremely dry times will they need to visit the nearby stream for a drink. The joey is 10 months old. He still tucks his head into his mother's pouch for an occasional sip of milk, but mostly he eats solid food. His strong sense of smell helps him choose the least toxic and most nourishing leaves.

cough-belch that can be heard more than half a mile (0.8 km) away. The louder the vocalization, the more powerful the male. The sound has a twofold purpose: it attracts females and warns off rivals. If a fight over territory breaks out, male koalas bite and claw each other until one gives up.

Once they are two or three years old, koalas can reproduce every year. The dominant male in a colony will father about half of the joeys born there. Other males travel around and mate with females before being chased away by the colony's dominant male. Having different fathers helps members of a koala colony remain genetically mixed, which is important for the health of the colony. Male koalas do

Vocal exercises

Male koalas have an extra pair of vocal cords called velar vocal folds (VVFs). VVFs allow koalas to produce sounds as deep and powerful as an elephant's. No other animals have VVFs.

(4) **YEARS**

‣ Settles near a colony
‣ Successfully mates for the first time

FEATURED  FAMILY

Practice Makes Perfect

At 13 months old, the young koala is now about half the size of his mother. He
has settled into the fork of a yellow gum tree. Not entirely comfortable with
his independence yet, he keeps an eye on his mother as she munches leaves
nearby. She has taught him to select only the best leaves, and he has mas-
tered the use of his tongue to pull the greenery toward his back teeth. Like his
mother, he will enjoy this crunchy meal for another half hour before drifting
off to sleep.

KOALA PREDATORS

WEDGE-TAILED EAGLE

DINGO

GOANNA

not participate in raising offspring. Mothers are solely responsible for protecting their joeys from danger. High in the trees, joeys that stray too far from their mothers may be attacked by pythons and goannas. The powerful owl, Australia's largest owl species, has a wingspan of more than four feet (1.2 m). The wedge-tailed eagle is nearly twice as big. Young koalas can become easy meals for these birds of prey.

(5) YEARS

▸ Fights dominant male
▸ Takes over territory

(12) YEARS

▸ End of life

CHAPTER FOUR

KOALA SPOTTING

Koalas are in serious trouble. In Queensland, 80 percent of koala habitat has been destroyed as a result of human expansion. Koalas are being pushed onto ever-smaller segments of land—often just a few trees between homes or alongside highways. As koalas travel in search of food and mates, they risk vehicle strikes and dog attacks. Hundreds of koalas are killed annually in urban areas. Another problem is inbreeding. Urbanization prevents koalas from traveling among colonies, forcing them to breed with the same individuals year after year. This causes an increase in illness and genetic disorders, which have led to a continued decline in koala populations.

In southern Australia, many national parks and protected areas, including islands, have been set aside for koalas. However, with few natural predators and a ban on hunting since the 1920s, koala numbers have exploded in relation to the food sources available to them. Instead of the ideal ratio of 1 koala per tree, some areas see up to 15 koalas feeding on a single tree. By eating all the available leaves, the koalas unintentionally kill the tree. Entire forests have been over-browsed by koalas, leading to the starvation of some colonies.

The Australian government has tried to manage southern koala habitats by capturing and moving koalas from place to place. These efforts have not been successful. There simply aren't enough places in southern Australia to move the koalas. Scientists do not want to move southern koalas northward, because southern koalas are not adapted to the warmer climate of northern Australia.

Only about 80,000 koalas exist in the wild. The Australian Koala Foundation warns that continued destruction of eucalyptus forests could cause koalas to die out by 2050. In urban areas, scientists work with city planners to plant trees on bridges and adapt tunnels under roadways. They hope to encourage koalas to follow such alternate paths. The citizens of Australia also regularly help koalas. Sick and injured koalas are cared for in hospitals, sanctuaries, and even private homes. People raise young koalas or rehabilitate animals that are then released back into the wild. But what koalas need most are safe places to live. Only when humans stop destroying and start recovering koala habitat will these marsupials have a chance at long-term survival.

SNAPSHOTS

In 1925, the San Diego Zoo's first **koalas**, Snugglepot and Cuddlepie, were presented as gifts from the children of Sydney, Australia.

In Victoria's You Yangs Regional Park, conservationists have planted thousands of trees to help restore **southern koala** habitat.

Born in 2017 at Australia Zoo in Queensland, **northern koala** Bert made several appearances on the Animal Planet show *Crikey! It's the Irwins.*

Northern koala Lizzy was hit by a car in 2015. Her joey, Phantom, refused to let go of her during surgery. Mom and joey were both released back into the wild about a month later.

PHANTOM

Because male **koalas** travel more and fight each other for better habitat, they tend to live only about 12 years. Females typically live a few years longer.

GOOLARA

San Diego Zoo's Goolara, born in 1985, was a rare albino **koala**—the first non-wild one known.

Leonard, a character in the Nickelodeon series *The Penguins of Madagascar*, is based on **northern koalas**.

By 1900, **southern koalas** had disappeared from the Narrandera region of New South Wales. Reintroduced in 1972, koalas there now number about 200.

The oldest koala on record was named Birthday Girl. The **southern koala** lived at the Port Macquarie Koala Hospital in New South Wales, where she died in 2011 at age 25.

Founded in 1927, Lone Pine Koala Sanctuary in Queensland is the world's oldest and largest koala sanctuary. Today, it houses about 130 **northern koalas**.

A **northern koala** breeding program at Riverbank Zoo in South Carolina began in 2003 with Lottie. She gave birth to 11 joeys at the zoo.

Established in 1892, Tower Hill Wildlife Reserve is Victoria's first national park. **Southern koalas** inhabit the forest around a 30,000-year-old volcano.

In 2016, Alethea and Tartar became the first two **northern koalas** to move into the Dreamworld Wildlife Foundation's Futurelab research facility.

WORDS to Know

adaptations   changes in a species that help it survive in a changed environment

albino   animals that have a genetic disorder that makes them all white with pink eyes

genetic   of or relating to genes (the basic units of heredity)

gland   an organ in an animal's body that produces chemical substances used by other parts of the body

mammals   animals that have a backbone and hair or fur, give birth to live young, and produce milk to feed their young

species   a group of living beings with shared characteristics and the ability to reproduce with one another

weaned   accustomed to food other than milk

LEARN MORE

Books

Eszterhas, Suzi. *Koala Hospital*. Berkeley, Calif.: Owlkids Books, 2015.

Gregory, Josh. *Koalas*. New York: Children's Press, 2016.

Sturm, Jeanne. *Marsupials*. Vero Beach, Fla.: Rourke Educational Media, 2013.

Websites

"Interesting Facts." Australian Koala Foundation. https://www.savethekoala
.com/about-koalas/interesting-facts.

"Koala." National Geographic. https://www.nationalgeographic.com/animals
/mammals/k/koala/.

"Koala." San Diego Zoo Animals & Plants. https://animals.sandiegozoo.org
/animals/koala.

Documentaries

Scott, Paul. "Cracking the Koala Code." *Nature*, season 30, episode 14. Wild
Fury Pty. Ltd./Thirteen WNET, 2012.

Scott, Paul. *Koalas: Slow Life in the Fast Lane*. Wild Fury, 2012.

Windemuth, Ellen. *Secret Life of the Koala*, 2 episodes. Smithsonian Earth, 2016.

Visit

PALM BEACH ZOO & CONSERVATION SOCIETY

The Koala Experience offers visitors a close-up view.

1301 Summit Boulevard
West Palm Beach, FL 33405

SAN DIEGO ZOO

Home to the largest koala colony outside Australia.

2920 Zoo Drive
San Diego, CA 92101

SAN FRANCISCO ZOO

The outdoor Koala Crossing exhibit has featured koalas since 1985.

Sloat Boulevard & Great Highway
San Francisco, CA 94132

ZOO MIAMI

Resident koalas Milo and Rinny launched a new breeding program in 2019.

12400 SW 152 Street
Miami, FL 33177

INDEX